POTATO CHIP BOOKS™

SO GOOD YOU CAN'T STOP READING THEM!

Back Seat Blues

Written by Marilyn Pitt
Illustrated by John Bianchi

9

Use the words you know to read new words!

eat	**look**
meat	took
beat	hook
seat	book

and	**five**
band	hive
land	dive
hand	drive

Put a __ on the front of the word. What word does that make?

all	b	f	t	h
an	c	m	p	St
it	f	p	s	sp

Take off the first letters. Put a __ in its place. What word does that make?

black	b	p	sn	tr
stop	h	m	t	sh
when	h	p	t	J

For more information, please visit
www.americanreadingathome.com

Tricky Words

any

more

right